Betrayed...

By My So-Called Friend

TANISHA STEWART

Prologue

June had listened to Kay'Ceon's lies for the last time.

"Come on baby," he was saying. He placed his hand over hers for emphasis as he gave her his now infamous puppy-dog look. It took everything in her power for June not to roll her eyes. "You know I would never do anything to intentionally hurt you."

This time she did roll her eyes, along with sucking her teeth. "Never do anything to hurt me, huh?" She snatched her hand away from his as he attempted to caress the back of her palm to calm her down. That always worked on her in the past - Kay'Ceon's gentle touch. Not today.

She whipped out her phone.

"What is this, Kay'Ceon?" She thrust the screenshot in his direction. "And don't lie."

She watched him carefully as he attempted to construct a lie to cover up what was showing on the phone's screen.

How could I not have seen this before? June was thoroughly disappointed in herself. *I should have listened to Camaiyah.*

Her heart panged as her eyes blurred with tears. Her best friend, Camaiyah, and even her sister Iliana, had both tried to convince June that Kay'Ceon was no good.

But she just refused to believe it until now.

It took the girl that he was messing with behind her back sending her direct messages between she and Kay'Ceon for June to finally see the light.

He was a liar, just like they tried to tell her.

He was talking again, but his words barely even fazed her.

"Look, I only came over here to tell you that we were through," she cut him off mid-sentence.

He opened his mouth to speak again, but she wasn't here for any more of his BS.

"I'm serious, Kay'Ceon. We're done. And this is the last time."

"Come on baby," Kay'Ceon said, repeating the same phrase he tried to use on her at the beginning of this conversation.

"Ugh," she sighed. She began to gather her things to go.

"So you really just gonna leave? We need to talk about this."

"Kay'Ceon, I'm not going in this circle with you anymore. We've been doing this back and forth thing, with you cheating on me and me taking you back, for far too long. It's gotten to the point where I have your lines memorized before you even say them. I'm done this time for real."

"June..." his voice trailed off as she stood and began walking toward the door.

"Save it. Have a nice life."

Before she walked out the door, she looked back at him one last time.

She could have sworn she saw a hint of sincerity in his eyes, but she was not repeating this toxic cycle yet again.

She was free.

***

June thought that the emotions she felt over she and Kay'Ceon's breakup would have died down by now, but two weeks later, she was still back and forth like a rollercoaster.

Some moments, she felt free like she felt when she walked out of his house, while at others, she desperately wanted to pick up the phone to call him just to hear his voice.

She hated when her mind went in that direction. One would think that after everything he put her through, she would never want to speak to him again.

But here she was, staring at his name on her contacts list.

She still hadn't found the strength to delete his number or block him.

She jolted as she heard a knock on her front door.

"Who is that?" she mumbled as she got up out of her seat to answer the door. She peeked through her curtains and saw that it was Iliana and Camaiyah - her sister and best friend.

"Hey y'all," she said when she opened the door to let them in.

"Hey boo!" said Camaiyah.

"Hey sis," said Iliana.

They each took a seat in June's living room. June and Iliana sat on the couch, while Camaiyah sat in the recliner.

It was then that June noticed the brown paper bag that Camaiyah was holding.

"I must have really been out of it," she said to Camaiayah. "What's in the bag?"

"Girl, what you think?" Camaiyah said, breaking out a bottle of Henny along with a bottle of blueberry Moscato. "It's time to get you out of this funk you been in."

June eyed the bottle of blueberry Moscato - her favorite drink.

"You know I've been trying to give up drinking."

Camaiyah rolled her eyes. "Don't be a Debbie Downer, June. We're doing this for you." She looked at Iliana.

Iliana gave June an encouraging smile. "Come on sis; one drink won't hurt."

"Right," Camaiyah added. "And besides, it's not like you was no alcoholic or nothing no way."

"Fine," June said, feeling herself loosen up a little. "Just one drink."

An entire bottle later, June was feeling pretty saucy. She and Iliana were giggling back and forth. Camaiyah was ironically the sober one, though she had downed the full bottle of Henny herself.

"Damn, Cam!" June slurred. "You could drink the both of us under the table."

Camaiyah rolled her eyes. "I'm glad you're feeling better. Even though it's at my expense."

"Oh... I'm so sorry little baby..." June attempted to soothe her. "I didn't mean to hurt your feelings."

Camaiyah burst out laughing. "Bitch you drunk as hell! I ain't mad at you though."

Iliana was busy bobbing her head to an imaginary beat.

"And look at this bitch," Camaiyah nudged June. "Fuck is she dancing to?"

She and Camaiyah shared another laugh at Iliana's expense, but Iliana was too zoned out to notice. She was the first to get drunk, always.

"Hey, so I have an idea," Camaiyah started.

"Girl, I am not flashing nobody tonight," June said. "I'm not that drunk." She was referring to the time they had a ladies' night at a hotel with a few other girls, and Camaiyah dared June to go in the hallway and flash some of the other patrons.

June obliged, but only because she was twisted out of her mind - it was during another one of she and Kay'Ceon's breakups. When she woke up the next morning with a hangover and a full description of what she had done the night before, she vowed at that moment never to drink again.

But here she was.

"Chill out - it's nothing like that," Camaiyah said. "It's just a little something to get your mind off Kay'Ceon."

"Something like what?"

"You ever heard of *Ready or Not*?

Ready or Not was a dating app that supposedly had great results when it came to hooking people up with prospective mates.

June wrinkled her nose.

"Ugh, no. I am turned off from all men right now."

Camaiyah sucked her teeth. "Come on. It's not like you have to marry none of them. Just get back out there and get your feet wet. See what the world has to offer besides Kay'Ceon."

Just then, Iliana cut into the conversation like she remembered something.

"That's right, sis! You need to get back out there."

"But y'all don't think it's too soon? It's literally only been two weeks."

"Girl, ain't no time limit on moving on. Not like he was bout shit anyway." Camaiyah shrugged her shoulders and grabbed June's phone from the coffee table.

She held it out to June.

"Unlock ya screen," she urged.

June stared at the phone for a second. She looked at Camaiyah, then Iliana's encouraging smile.

"Fine," she said, taking the phone. "But I'm not taking any of these guys seriously."

An hour later, June's profile, fully equipped with pictures, was up and running.

She scrolled through the site looking to see if there were any cute guys on there.

Her eyes widened as she saw a notification at the top of her screen.

She clicked on it and her jaw dropped when she saw what it led to.

"What?" said Camaiyah, who had been eyeing her for a few moments.

"Twenty messages already?" June said in shock.

"Twenty messages?!" Camaiyah sounded like she couldn't believe her ears.

"Yes, Souljah Boy," June rolled her eyes. She held out her phone for Camaiyah and Iliana to see. "All from different guys, too."

"Girl, you poppin!" Iliana sang. "Get it, sis!"

A strange look crossed Camaiyah's face. "Right. You LIT."

After Camaiyah and Iliana had fallen asleep, June found herself scrolling once again through the dating app.

She was amazed at how many messages she was receiving in such little time. It was hard keeping up with responding to so many people all at once, but it definitely made her feel a boost of confidence.

"Camaiyah was right," she breathed.

The next day, June told Camaiyah and Iliana all about her messages between the different men over breakfast.

"I mean, of course I'm not thinking of anything serious at the moment," June was saying. "But I really am happy you guys convinced me to sign up."

"I say go on a few dates," said Iliana. She looked so happy for her sister.

They both looked at Camaiyah, but she seemed to barely be paying attention to the conversation.

"Are you okay?" June asked.

"Yeah, I'm good. Just got a headache."

"Oh, you should have eaten something before you started drinking," said June.

"Right."

June continued with the site for a few more days.

The excitement over all of those messages was starting to wear off - a lot of those dudes reminded her of Kay'Ceon.

When she expressed this to Iliana and Camaiyah, they urged her to just keep going.

So she did.

And good thing she listened, yet again, because less than 24 hours later, she received her first message from Jermaine.

She could immediately tell that he was different from the way that he approached her. He stood out from all the rest.

The next three months practically flew by as June and Jermaine's conversations grew more and more. The whole concept of online dating was intriguing for June - all the other guys she had dated, she met them in person - including Kay'Ceon.

But things with Jermaine were totally different.

They were taking things very slow, something else that was new for June.

They were building up to their very first phone conversation...

June couldn't wait til they were official, just so she could rub it in Kay'Ceon's stupid face.

It got all the way down to the day June and Jermaine were supposed to have their very first phone conversation.

June got all dressed up and everything, even though she knew Jermaine wouldn't be able to see her through the phone.

At the time that they agreed to do the call, June sent Jermaine a message on the *Ready or Not* app to get his number - in all her excitement, she missed that very important detail.

...But Jermaine never wrote back.

In fact, she checked her notifications every ten minutes for hours - he never even logged in to see the message.

At first she thought he was just busy, or nervous about finally talking on the phone with her for the first time.

But when she saw that he had went a full 24 hours without being online, she felt like something might be wrong.

By day two, she was getting frantic.

What happened to Jermaine???

Betrayed...

By My So-Called Friend

Chapter 1

June stared at her phone, tapping her foot impatiently to the rhythm of the three little dots as she waited for the text from her best guy friend, Kelvin, to come through. It finally announced its arrival with a text ping.

I have something to tell you. It's about Jermaine.

As soon as she saw that, her pulse quickened.

She fired back a reply, her thumbs flying across the keyboard. *Did something happen? What's wrong with Jermaine?*

As soon as she sent the text, it hit her how odd this was. *Why is Kelvin messaging me about Jermaine?*

Across town in his own kitchen, Kelvin read June's frantic reply and started typing a text to finally tell her the truth, but before he could hit the Send arrow, a call beeped in from June's trifling best friend, Camaiyah.

He was ready to curse her out, and his finger hesitated over the Accept button to answer the call. He rolled his eyes and sighed. That girl had a lot of nerve calling him. Just the other day he had caught her and Iliana, June's sister, catfishing June using Jermaine's name and profile. He couldn't believe they had done something like this, knowing how vulnerable and gullible June was when it came to men. Kelvin finally had the proof that would settle the score once and for all, and he planned to lay it out for Camaiyah so straight that she would have no doubt how he felt about her dirty little tricks.

"What?" he answered.

"Before you go snitching to June, you should know that we are not the only ones who have dirty hands in this situation." The evil glee in Camaiyah's voice was unmistakable. She might as well have been cackling like a witch, it was so obvious.

Kelvin snorted, ready to call her bluff. "What could you possibly have on me?"

"Exhibit A," said Iliana, who was obviously leaning close to Camaiyah's phone to be part of the conversation, as she always did. A text pinged Kelvin's phone.

When he saw it, his mouth fell open. "Y'all were recording?!?"

"Yeah, boy, you're my bitch now. How you like that?" This time Camaiyah actually did cackle like an evil little witch.

He immediately felt his insides kick into overdrive. He couldn't possibly tell June now, not with the information Camaiyah and Iliana were holding over his head. He stood frozen in place, contemplating if there was a way out of this trap. *I got nothing*, he thought. *If June sees that video, she'll never speak to me again, much less want me to be her man*. He sucked his teeth and sighed. He would just have to settle for being a second to Jermaine.

And the most fucked up part about it is, Jermaine's not even a real person.

***

Kelvin's mind traveled back to the day he met June.

It was the first day of their junior year of college. They had both transferred to the four-year school from different community colleges.

June didn't have any friends on campus, since Camaiyah pursued a massage therapy program rather than a degree and already had a job, and Iliana was still in high school.

Kelvin saw June looking nervous as her eyes shot from building to building on the huge campus. It was clear that she was lost.

"Hey," he said, staring at her and licking his lips. For most other guys, this would have been seen as a smooth gesture, but for Kelvin, it likely looked awkward, like he had forgotten his chap stick that day or something. "You looking for something?"

June looked up at him. "Um... Yes. I'm trying to find the registrar?"

Her soft brown eyes had him mesmerized, but Kelvin fought to remain focused.

"Oh - I literally just left the registrar. I can walk you there. Are you signing up for classes?"

Obviously, Kel, his brain screamed at him.

"Oh, no. I already signed up. I just need them to print out my schedule for me."

"Oh." Kelvin felt more and more embarrassed by the second. "Well, you know you can look up your schedule online, right?"

"I do, but I still like to have a physical copy."

"Okay... Well, I'll lead the way."

June's smile sent butterflies all through Kelvin's stomach.

As they walked, she kept looking down and smiling at her phone.

"Don't mind me," said June. "Just going back and forth with my boyfriend, Kay'Ceon."

Kelvin almost stopped in his tracks at those words. *Boyfriend?! Shit, Kel. You sure know how to pick them.*

Kelvin walked June the rest of the way to the registrar's office.

Once she got her schedule, they found out that they had three classes together.

From that moment on, their friendship blossomed.

Every time June broke up with Kay'Ceon, Kelvin wanted to make a move, but before he could, she always ended up back together with him.

Once they finally broke up for good, Kelvin tried to give her some space before he approached her.

But then she started talking about Jermaine.

Kelvin kicked himself every day for the past few months as June and Jermaine's relationship continued to grow stronger.

Until the things she was telling him about Jermaine stopped making sense.

What guy in their right mind waits months to have a phone conversation with a woman he is really into? Why was there no effort to FaceTime? No plans for them to meet up in person?

Things started to sound really fishy to Kelvin, so he felt the need to investigate.

Once he did, he found out the truth.

Now the only thing left to do was to break June's heart with the news.

***

"Umm … WTH, Kelvin??" June saw the three dots disappear like he'd changed his mind and deleted the text he was sending. She couldn't believe this! Right when it was about to get good. "Ugh, he stay leaving me hanging. Playing with my emotions and ish." That boy got on her last nerve sometimes. He was known to literally stop mid-sentence as if he'd forgotten what he was talking about, and not remember again until at least three days later. It was usually when he was sharing something juicy, too.

Not this time. I'm not about to sit around for three whole days waiting for Kelvin's brain to catch up with his fingers.

She needed to know what the deal was with Jermaine, and Kelvin obviously knew what was up. She felt like she was falling hard for Jermaine, even though they had only talked online. They hadn't even facetimed each other yet, but still, she knew that what they had was real. Jermaine was the first man she had ever met that she felt knew her before they even spoke. He reached out to her on a dating app that she signed up for on a whim.

Camaiyah and Iliana had pestered her to sign up for the app, claiming that she needed to "get with the times and get her a new man." She was totally surprised to discover that

Jermaine was so sweet—a far cry from her first love turned ex, Kay'Ceon, who had broken her heart in ways one could only imagine.

Kelvin was really working her nerves here. She hoped that he didn't have any bad news about Jermaine.

Hellooooo! she texted him, tapping her foot against the floor.

She silently prayed that he hadn't had a brain freeze and forgotten what he was about to tell her.

She stirred her pasta as she waited for his response, glancing at her phone every few seconds.

"Come on, Kelvin, get your brain in gear, boy!"

Three hours later, there was still no word from Kelvin.

"Forget this. I need answers." She threw on her shoes and coat, locked the front door behind her, and headed to Kelvin's house.

***

"Shoot! Shoot! Shoot! She's on her way!" Kelvin was frantic as he tracked June's location through her social media app. Hey, he knew it was low-key stalkerish, but he had to buy time somehow. Unfortunately, though, it seemed that the jig was up: June was on her way to his house, and from the tracker on the app, it showed she was only five minutes away.

"Think quick, Kel! Think quick!" He paced back and forth, nervously licking his lips as he ran one hand over the back of his head.

Why didn't I just write her back? I could have played it off.

Only four minutes remained until June would be at his house.

He knew that what he was about to do was extremely childish, but he felt he had no other option.

With two minutes remaining until June's arrival, he hopped in his whip and bounced.

Chapter 2

Meanwhile, Iliana and Camaiyah were busy turning up. "We got that nigga, bih!" Camaiyah said in a singsong voice.

"I can't believe this has been going on for so long," Iliana said, playing it cool and casual, but she was really throwing out feelers to see how Camaiyah felt about this catfish situation. It had started out as a harmless joke that somehow turned into a cruel prank, but Camaiyah seemed to be enjoying it almost too much.

Iliana had put on a front over the phone, but she was secretly hoping Kelvin wouldn't tell June what was really going on. She didn't even know how he'd found out that she and Camaiyah were catfishing her.

If June found out that her own sister was involved in something like this, much less her best friend, the consequences would be unbearable.

"Maybe we should just tell June," said Iliana, pacing her shots so that she only took one for every three that Camaiyah knocked back.

"Whatchu mean? This is CLASSIC!" Camaiyah slammed down her shot glass, poured another, and kicked it back. "Baby girl ain't gonna know what hit her when she finds out."

Iliana chuckled and finally took half a shot. "So how much longer should we let this play out before we come clean?"

Camaiyah wrinkled her nose. "Come clean? Never. Let her figure it out!"

"And how is she going to do that? From all the messages we've been sending, she thinks Jermaine is real, Cam! What are we going to do when she finds out? Plus, we got Kelvin on our backs now too! This is gonna blow up soon, and when it does—"

"Pshht, Kelvin ain't 'bout to do shit. Trust me, I got him."

"You say that, but you forget that he's her best friend too."

"Okay, but I've known her longer."

"Camaiyah, he has proof that it was us."

Camaiyah flipped her hand at Iliana like she was swatting a fly that kept coming at her. "Okay, so what? He's not going to use it. And why are you so worried all of a sudden now anyway? Don't tell me you getting scared."

"Nobody's scared. I'm just trying to figure out what the end game is."

"The end game is letting June know that she can't have everything she wants." Camaiyah's tone was so cold that Iliana had to just stare at her to see if she was serious.

"What is that supposed to mean?" she said.

Camaiyah had never let Iliana fully in on her reasons for catfishing June, who supposedly was her best friend. The reason? June had "stolen" Camaiyah's man, Kay'Ceon, back in tenth grade. *Well, he technically wasn't my man yet, but June had to have known that I had my eyes on him first.*

Camaiyah thought back to that day...

Kay'Ceon was leaning against his locker, sporting brand new all white Air Force's. He looked good enough to eat, and Camaiyah was hungry for him.

They hadn't really spoken to each other, but ever since Camaiyah saw him on the first day of school, she was caught up. They had the same homeroom together.

Today was the day that all of that was about to change, however.

Camaiyah slowly made her way up to where Kay'Ceon was standing.

He was wearing a white fitted cap, which accentuated his thick, full, juicy looking lips. It was against the rules to wear hats, of course, and Principal Henry was bound to make him take it off, so Camaiyah was taking full advantage of the view of his sexiness while it lasted.

OMG, I'm in love, she breathed.

She stopped in front of him. Their eyes met and her heart dropped. At that moment, she realized that she hadn't prepared any words for what she was supposed to say to him.

"Hey Camaiyah," he said, and his voice was like music to her ears.

She felt her face redden. *He knows my name?!?* Camaiyah blushed and opened her mouth to respond, but June waltzed up to them, full of attitude.

"Girl, listen. Principal Henry is no joke. She just threatened to send me home, claiming my skirt was too short! So unfair. Ugh!"

Camaiyah fought to keep her attention on Kay'Ceon, but it was clear that it was no use. His eyes were now traveling up and down June's bare legs, taking in the shortness of her miniskirt.

"Damn," he breathed.

Camaiyah's heart dropped again, this time for an entirely different reason.

June didn't seem to notice that Kay'Ceon was practically salivating in her direction. She was too busy waiting for Camaiyah to respond to her disdain for Principal Henry.

"Damn Ma," Kay'Ceon repeated. "I don't think we've been introduced. What's your name?"

It was at that moment that June finally realized that Kay'Ceon was trying to get her attention.

Her eyes softened as she took in his features, and the chemistry between them was obvious.

Camaiyah felt mute as they carried on a full conversation right in front of her face.

She barely felt like she was even there...

Camaiyah snapped out of her reverie when she heard Iliana still expressing her concern over June.

She didn't say what she was thinking, but she opened her mouth to give a deflecting non-answer when a loud, urgent knock at the front door stopped her cold.

Iliana's head whipped around. "Who's that?"

***

June stood outside Iliana's house, heated. She had just been to Kelvin's house to see what was going on, but he wasn't home. She felt like something was up with that, because Kelvin was usually home on Thursdays. Besides, he was the

27

one who dropped the text bomb about Jermaine, then he went silent, then he was gone by the time she went to his house. What was going on?

She banged on Iliana's door again. "Come on, open the door," she muttered.

"Hey, sis!" Iliana greeted her.

June walked in and gave her a hug. "Hey, girl. Hey, Camaiyah."

"Wassup?" said Camaiyah from the kitchen, a huge grin on her face. She was on her eighth shot now, and somehow was still standing.

"Y'all turning up already?" June eyed the bottles scattered all over the kitchen table.

"Yesss, bih! No work tomorrow!" Camaiyah sang.

Iliana chuckled. "She already tipsy, girl."

June grinned and started to say something sarcastic, but she saw a hint of uneasiness in her sister's eyes.

"What's up?" she said. "Come on, I know you too well. You're not telling me something, and now Kelvin's acting all weird on me."

Iliana's gaze shifted, and she shrugged her shoulders. "It's nothing. Just worried about these finals." Iliana was in her last semester at the local community college.

June smiled, proud of her younger sister. "Don't worry about it, Sis. You got this."

Iliana smiled. "Thanks. Where you coming from?"

"Girl, Kelvin's house!" June sighed and made her way over to the couch to sit down.

"Oh, really?" said Iliana, staring at her intently. "What were y'all doing over there?" Her jealousy was obvious.

June stared at her sister. *She really got it bad.* Iliana had been secretly crushing on Kelvin forever. June had only found out by stumbling upon Iliana's diary a few months back. She felt guilty about reading her sister's private thoughts without her permission, but when she saw Kelvin's name as she flipped through the pages, she had to pause. She read that entry, but forced herself not to read any more.

June knew she had to tread carefully not to get Iliana all stirred up. "Nothing happened. He wasn't even there. He messaged me earlier saying he had something to tell me, but when I tried to find out what it was, he started to write back, but then no text came through."

Iliana rolled her eyes to play it off. "That's Kelvin for you." She let out a little laugh.

"So, how's things with Jermaine?" said Camaiyah, shooting her a mischievous grin as she sauntered in from the kitchen holding three shot glasses in her hands. She handed one to

Iliana, and held one out to June, but June declined.

"Girl, you know I don't drink no more." June shook her head an emphatic no.

Camaiyah rolled her eyes. "Yeah, that's right. You too good to turn up now."

"Camaiyah, you know it's not even like that." June sighed. "It's just—"

Her phone vibrated in her back pocket. She whipped it out. "Finally!" She said, swiping to answer the call.

"Who is that?" said Iliana, looking nervous all over again.

"Kelvin."

June pressed the phone to her ear. "Boy, where'd you go tonight? I came by your house when you never replied to my text. I need to know what's going on."

June noticed that both Camaiyah and Iliana were giving her strange looks when she answered the phone, but she shrugged them off and focused on her conversation with Kelvin.

Kelvin scrambled to think of a good excuse. He didn't want her to find out about the video. He was drunk when it was made, but that didn't take away from the things he said about her in it. He honestly hadn't known that Iliana and Camaiyah were recording their conversation that night, and he knew they had probably edited out the things they'd said about June to make him look bad. They had spent a good hour roasting her about everything from her uppity attitude to the fact that she couldn't keep a man to save her life, and if that wasn't bad enough, they had talked trash about her looks.

Kelvin hadn't meant most of the things he'd said, but June wouldn't see it that way. *If June sees that video, she will hate me.*

"Hello-o-o?" she said, nudging him to respond.

Kelvin realized that he just couldn't do it. He wasn't ready to face the consequences, and he knew she would be so angry that she would never speak to him again.

"Let me call you right back." He hung up before she could get another word in.

June stared at the phone in shock.

She looked at Iliana and Camaiyah, who were both still staring at her like they were holding their breath or something.

"I know this nigga did not just call me, then hang up on me!"

Camaiyah spoke first. "Girl, you know Kelvin's square ass be doing weird shit all the time. I wouldn't even worry about it."

"Right," Iliana jumped in. "He does that to me all the time too."

"That's easy for you guys to say when he isn't holding onto critical information!" June wanted to pull her hair out.

What information did Kelvin have about Jermaine???

"Damn, Kel!" he cussed himself out. *Why am I making this so difficult?*

He knew the answer before the question shot through his thoughts. He didn't want to lose her. Despite all the things he said in that video, he loved June—really loved her. That was one of the reasons he decided to investigate this dude Jermaine in the first place. June had always been gullible when it came to men, so when she mentioned endearing little things that Jermaine said or did, coupled with the fact that Jermaine never seemed to get around to actually meeting her, Kelvin used his tech skills to get to the bottom of it.

His suspicions proved true.

When he found out that Iliana and Camaiyah were catfishing June, posing as Jermaine, he was heated, to say the least, but not surprised. Iliana wasn't really the type to do something like this, but Camaiyah had always been jealous of June, as far as he knew. Iliana was more of a follower.

He tried to warn June many times about Camaiyah, but she never listened. She just

32

brushed it off, claiming that Camaiyah was her "ride or die," and they were basically sisters. He knew she would be devastated to find out that she had been betrayed by her so-called friend.

His cell phone rang with a call from June, breaking him out of his thoughts once again. He knew he would have to answer; he couldn't run for the rest of his life.

"Hello?" he said, his heart pounding.

"Kelvin, if you do not stop playing on my phone...!" She was clearly heated. "What did you want to tell me earlier?"

"Listen. We need to meet up."

"Meet up where, Kelvin? I already went by your house earlier, but you weren't there. You're usually home on Thursdays. Where are you?"

He paused. "I'm actually home now."

"Okay, so where were you? You left me hanging for three hours!"

"Just come over my house. I'll be here." He didn't have time to make any more excuses.

"Okay. And you better be there too."
CLICK.

Chapter 3

June sucked her teeth. Kelvin was getting on her last nerve with his suspicious behavior. "I'll see you guys later," she said to Iliana and Camaiyah, and made her way to the door.

"Wait, where you going?" said Iliana, grabbing her arm.

"Didn't you just hear me on the phone? Kelvin said he's finally home, so I have to find out what's up with Jermaine."

"Okay, but do you have to leave right now?"

Something about Camaiyah's expression made June wonder what was going on.

"Um, yes. He sounded like it was important."

"It's probably not though, knowing Kelvin." It was obvious that Iliana was hiding something.

"Why are y'all so heavy on my back about this? Jermaine hasn't responded to my messages in two days. I need to find out what's going on with him, and it sounds like Kelvin knows something. Wouldn't you want to find out if Jermaine was your man?"

Iliana and Camaiyah shared a side-eye glance, but June caught it. She turned to face them both head on, her hands planted at her hips. "What's going on? Come on, out with it. I know you both too well for you to pretend like it's nothing."

"What do you mean?" said Iliana, looking uneasy.

"Why are you guys so tense? Why don't you want me to go over Kelvin's house?"

"It's not that we don't want you to go," said Camaiyah. "It's that you just got here with us, but now you running off to go see about Jermaine. You never have time for us anymore."

June couldn't believe her ears. "Where's this guilt-tripping coming from? I talk to you guys almost every day, and we see each other every weekend! I've never even met Jermaine in person, so excuse me if I feel like I need to know what Kelvin wants to tell me."

"Don't you think there's a reason for that?" Iliana blurted before she could stop herself.

"For what?"

Camaiyah shot a warning look in Iliana's direction. There was no way she was about to snitch in her presence. "Nothing, girl," she said to June. "Go. Iliana is just mad that you're leaving so soon."

June rolled her eyes. "Whatever. I'll see you two after I finish with Kelvin."

Iliana watched through the window blinds as June got in her car to head to Kelvin's house. She turned back to Camaiyah. "So we're just going to let her go?"

Camaiyah shrugged, a little too nonchalantly for Iliana's liking. "What were we supposed to do, hold her hostage?"

Iliana's mind swirled with thoughts. How was she going to get out of this one? Usually, she went to June for advice on how to get out of sticky situations, but now June was in the middle of her drama. She should have listened to June all those times she warned her about being a follower. She had been so caught up in trying to be down with Camaiyah that she hadn't seen her for who she truly was: a snake.

The night that they all got drunk and made that video, it was Camaiyah's idea to secretly record Kelvin. They were all acting a fool, taking turns making jokes at June's expense, all because she refused to hang with them. She was out on a date with Kay'Ceon, her on-again, off-again boyfriend since high school. To Iliana, they were all just joking around, but she knew that if June saw the video of Kelvin, she would think otherwise.

"Come on Iliana," Camaiyah had said the night of the recording. "This shit bout to be funny as hell."

"I don't know, Camaiyah. You know how Kelvin gets when he is drunk. He is way too loose with his tongue."

Camaiyah shrugged in indifference. "Okay, and that's our problem how? As long as we don't say nothing too bad, we good."

"Yeah, but..." Iliana didn't want to betray the true reason of her reluctance in this situation.

"Look, are you gonna do it or not?" Camaiyah was growing impatient.

"Not. Sorry. I have to pass on this one."

"OMG, whyyyy?" Camaiyah drew out her word.

"Because, Cam! How would you feel if someone recorded you without your knowledge?"

"It's just a fucking joke, Iliana. Damn. We'll delete it right after."

Iliana thought for a few more moments before she gave in.

They went through with the recording. At first it was all in fun, with each of them taking turns roasting June, but then Camaiyah took it a little further, and Kelvin followed suit. They all knew he didn't mean the things he was saying, but it certainly didn't look that way once Camaiyah edited the video.

Once Iliana saw the edited version, she tried to get Camiayah to delete it, but of course, she refused.

"We just gonna have a little fun with it first," Camaiyah had said, but she didn't sound reassuring at all.

To be completely honest, not only did Iliana want out of this situation because of her sister, but also because she wanted to protect Kelvin. She had been crushing on him since the first day that June introduced him to her, but she never told him how she felt. She was afraid that he would just see her as June's little sister rather than a love interest, so that's why she started hanging with June and Camaiyah more heavily. She wanted Kelvin to see her as a worthy prospect, but unfortunately, that ship was sunk. Kelvin would never want her now.

"Hello?" Camaiyah snapped her fingers in Iliana's face.

"What?"

"Did you hear anything I just said? I got a plan, bih!" Camaiyah's evil grin was back in place.

"What's your plan this time, Cam?"

"We're going to get him before he gets us." Camaiyah grabbed her purse and keys and hustled to the door.

Iliana followed, but she wished she never got herself into this mess. Now she had no choice but to roll with it.

***

June pulled up to Kelvin's house, glad to see that his car was parked outside. She walked up to the front door, her anticipation building with each step. She hoped that whatever he had to say about Jermaine wasn't bad, especially since she'd had nothing but silence from Jermaine in two days.

She was really looking forward to meeting the man of her dreams, and was convinced it would happen soon. It had to! Jermaine seemed like he really understood her and knew everything about her. If anything bad happened to him, she didn't know what she would do.

Kelvin was always on her back about rushing into things too quickly with guys, but she couldn't help it. She was a hopeless romantic who was just trying to find her one true love.

She knocked on the door and composed her expression so she didn't look too desperate. When Kelvin opened the door, she searched his face for clues, but got nothing. He closed the door behind them, then turned to face her, his expression unreadable.

Feeling awkward just standing there, she took a seat on his couch. "So?" she said, and waited. "About Jermaine..."

Kelvin was being way too silent for her liking. Usually he looked excited when she came by his house, and they were always laughing and joking about something.

Kelvin felt like he was going to choke. Here she was, the love of his life, and he was about to break her heart. *Why did she have to go on that site anyway? This whole time I've been standing right in front of her, but she never even saw me.* That was when it hit him. He was selfish. June was clearly sitting on pins and needles about some dude she didn't even know, but all he could think about was his own feelings.

"Listen, this is not gonna be easy what I have to say, but you deserve to know." He strode to the couch and sat down next to her.

June studied his features for clues. His expression was way too grim for this to be good news. *What could he possibly have to say about Jermaine? Did he know him from somewhere? Was he in an accident?* Her mind was frantic as Kelvin sat there staring at her, looking like he didn't know what to say.

"Kelvin, what is it? You're scaring me. I haven't heard from Jermaine in over two days. What do you know about him?"

Kelvin backed slightly away from June on the couch as if he was bracing himself for the blow she was about to take. It wasn't a pretty situation, but she needed to know. It was better for her to find out now than to fall even deeper for this guy.

"Jermaine's not—"

At that moment, they heard rapid footsteps thundering up the steps to his front porch, and loud fists banging on the front door.

"What the hell?" said June, her eyes darting from Kelvin to the door.

Chapter 4

"Hold on." Kelvin hopped up from the couch to see who was causing such a ruckus. He was not trying to deal with complaints from his neighbors. His landlord already couldn't stand him, but that was a problem for another day.

He whipped open the door, ready to cuss out whoever was on the other side when his jaw dropped.

Camaiyah pushed past him as she and Iliana strode into the middle of his living room.

June just sat there looking at them in confusion. "Camaiyah, did you drive here?" she finally said. "Are you crazy? Girl, you know you already got two DUIs, plus you got my baby sister in the car. What's wrong with you?"

"So you think you slick, huh?" Camaiyah said, whipping her head toward Kelvin, completely ignoring June.

"I think I'm slick? Why are you here, Camaiyah?" He could feel the heat rising within him. He could not stand this girl. He had seen her snake-like tendencies the moment June introduced them, but she was part of June's circle, whether he liked it or not, so he put up with her. Now she had gotten him into a situation that he didn't know how to handle. Basically, he was going down no matter how the story went. If he snitched, Camaiyah would flip.

"Yeah, what are y'all doing here?" June jumped back into the conversation. "I told you that I was coming back over to your house after I finished talking with Kelvin!"

"Okay, simmer down." Camaiyah didn't have to be so dramatic, trying to silence June with her hands, but she was feeling the shots she'd downed earlier. "What were you two talking about?" She looked back and forth between June and Kelvin.

June felt her blood pressure rising, so she got up off the couch to literally stand her ground. "What does it matter, Camaiyah? I told you that I was coming here so he could tell me what happened with Jermaine. Why are you so concerned? Why are you blocking?" She looked at Kelvin for help, but his expression was stony. She shot a glance at Iliana, who looked like she was about to piss on herself, and she looked at Camaiyah, who appeared to be low-key enjoying this moment. No one seemed to understand her anxiety. She just needed to know if Jermaine was okay, and why he hadn't answered her messages in two days.

"What's going on with Jermaine?" she demanded.

Kelvin said, "Look, June. I know you don't want to hear this, but—"

"So you think you just gonna do this right now, in front of both of us?" said Camaiyah, cutting him off.

"Yes, I am. This ends today." His tone was final.

"What is going on here?" said June, her voice rising.

"You are so fucking corny, Kel," said Camaiyah, brushing off June like she wasn't there. She was beyond irritated that he was really going to snitch like his hands were clean. This whole catfish thing was just getting good. Why stop now? June was telling "Jermaine" things that she'd never even told Camaiyah, and it was entertaining as hell.

"I'm corny?" Kelvin was taken aback. "Okay, so I'm corny, but you're the one acting like you auditioning for a damn reality show with your dramatic ass."

Camaiyah thought fast—anything to throw Kelvin off his square. "Oh, so I'm dramatic? Why is your best friend a female?"

"If you trying to insinuate something, you can just come out and say it!"

It worked! Camaiyah's evil grin told him that he had taken the bait.

June couldn't take it anymore. "Both of y'all, shut the hell up and tell me what happened to Jermaine!"

Iliana had just stood there silent as Kelvin and Camaiyah went at each other. She felt bad for her sister, though. June looked so desperate, crying out for answers, with nobody listening. Iliana couldn't take it anymore. It was time to come clean.

"Jermaine's not real!" They all whipped their heads toward her.

June's face went from shock, to anger, to hurt, all in a matter of seconds. "What did you just say?" Then she looked from Iliana to Camaiyah, from Camaiyah to Kelvin, and from Kelvin back to Iliana. She put two and two together as she took in their guilty eyes, all of them.

"Oh I get it now. I see what you've been doing." She shook her head at her own gullibility. "You're telling me that Jermaine isn't real. Is that true?" She looked at Kelvin. He nodded and swallowed, not taking his eyes off of her.

She pinned her gaze on Iliana and Camaiyah. "So how do you two factor in? How do all three of you know that Jermaine isn't real? How am I the last person to find out?"

Here she was in a living room with three of the people who were closest to her on earth, and they all seemed to know something that very deeply pertained to her life, but somehow, she was out of the loop. This was unreal.

The only possible explanation was that someone in this room had betrayed her. She sank onto the couch, her head spinning with the possibilities.

She looked at Iliana, but with a different set of eyes. *You're my sister.* Iliana knew more than anyone all the heartbreak June had been through over the years with different guys, each time thinking she'd found the one, each time being disappointed. They all turned out to be the same. They used her and abused her, and she was left to pick up the pieces.

A tear rolled down Iliana's cheek. "I'm sorry, June." She looked like she wanted to hug her, but she just stood there.

Camaiyah's expression was blank. She looked slightly unbothered by the fact that her best friend's heart was breaking before her eyes.

Kelvin looked torn. He was hurt to see her hurt, but his eyes told her there was more to the story. June wanted to press all of them for information, but it already hurt enough to find out that the man that she had poured her heart into for several months wasn't even a real person. *How could they play with my emotions like this? Whose idea was this? Who have I really been talking to this whole time?*

She recalled with pained embarrassment all of the sensitive details about her life that she had divulged to Jermaine. She needed answers.

She crossed her arms and sat back, putting on her poker face. "So, who was it? Or was it all of you?"

Kelvin knew June's poker face very well. She was trying to put on a front like she wasn't hurt, but he could see right through her. Jermaine had meant a lot to her—he could tell by the way she spoke about him, and how excited she became whenever he texted or messaged her. He was beginning to regret sending her that text saying he had something to tell her about Jermaine. *She would have found out eventually anyway that this dude wasn't real.* As soon as he had that thought, he regretted it. If he hadn't told her, he would've been no better than Camaiyah. He had to tell her.

He shot Camaiyah a look of disgust. He hated everything this girl represented. He couldn't for the life of him understand why June continued to trust her after she had shown sign after sign of not being loyal. He bet June still didn't know that Camaiyah had slept with Kay'Ceon while he was supposedly June's boyfriend! Kelvin had found out this juicy tidbit while he was compiling info on "Jermaine." Once he discovered that it was Camaiyah and Iliana doing the catfishing, he hacked both of their computers to pull messages. He saw the messages between Iliana and Camaiyah, as well as several conversations between Camaiyah and Kay'Ceon.

To make matters worse, the things he said that drunken night didn't even compare to the things Camaiyah said to Kay'Ceon about June. If June ever found out, he would need help picking Camaiyah up off the floor.

And Iliana—the poor girl was so lost. He had gleaned from the messages that she was all in on the idea of catfishing June in the beginning, but only because she thought it was a harmless joke. She had dropped little hints here and there that she and Camaiyah should stop, but she hadn't realized that Camaiyah was out to hurt June, and she was dragging June's baby sister right along with her, a casualty of war.

Kelvin couldn't ignore June's eyes imploring them for answers. Somebody had to say something soon.

"Don't everybody speak at once," said June. She folded her arms and braced herself for the worst.

Kelvin decided there was only one way out of this situation. What he was about to do might seem stupid to some, but he felt he had no other choice. He was partially to blame, so he might as well own it, and if he fessed up, maybe June would give him points for being honorable.

Iliana opened her mouth to speak, but Kelvin held up his hand to stop her.

"I got this, Iliana." He looked straight at June, his best friend, the love of his life, and hoped she would see the sincerity in his eyes.

"It was me, June. I'm Jermaine."

Dear Reader,

Many were angry with me at the end of this read (lol). This was originally a short story that was meant to be a standalone, but due to popular demand, it became a series.

If you are hungry for more, you may be excited to find that the saga between June and her friends (or lack thereof)

continues in <u>Betrayed... By My So-Called Friend, Part 2</u>.

PS: If you enjoyed this story, I would greatly appreciate it if you left a rating or review. Also, join my readers group on Facebook: <u>Tanisha Stewart Readers</u>!

Until next time,

Tanisha Stewart

Tanisha Stewart's Books

Even Me Series
Even Me
Even Me, The Sequel
Even Me, Full Circle

When Things Go Series
When Things Go Left
When Things Get Real
When Things Go Right

For My Good Series
For My Good: The Prequel
For My Good: My Baby Daddy Ain't Ish
For My Good: I Waited, He Cheated
For My Good: Torn Between The Two
For My Good: You Broke My Trust
For My Good: Better or Worse
For My Good: Love and Respect
Rick and Sharmeka: A BWWM Romance

Betrayed Series
Betrayed By My So-Called Friend
Betrayed By My So-Called Friend, Part 2
Betrayed 3: Camaiyah's Redemption
Betrayed Series: Special Edition
*Spin-offs coming soon!

Phate Series
Phate: An Enemies to Lovers Romance
Phate 2: An Enemies to Lovers Romance
Leisha & Manuel: Love After Pain

The Real Ones Series
Find You A Real One: A Friends to Lovers Romance
Find You A Real One 2: A Friends to Lovers Romance
Janie & E: Life Lessons

Standalones
A Husband, A Boyfriend, & a Side Dude
In Love With My Uber Driver
You Left Me At The Altar
Where. Is. Haseem?! A Romantic-Suspense Comedy
Caught Up With The 'Rona: An Urban Sci-Fi Thriller
#DOLO: An Awkward, Non-Romantic Journey Through Singlehood
December 21st: An Urban Supernatural Suspense
Should Have Thought Twice: A Psychological Thriller
Everybody Ain't Your Friend
The Maintenance Man